KT-214-709

For the Bear himself
V.P.

British Library Cataloguing in Publication Data
A catalogue record of this book is available from the British Library.

ISBN 0 340 80597 8 (HB)
ISBN 0 340 80598 6 (PB)

Text copyright © Vic Parker 2002
Illustrations copyright © Emily Bolam 2002

The right of Vic Parker to be identified as the author
and Emily Bolam as the illustrator of this Work
has been asserted by them in accordance with
the Copyright, Designs and Patents Act 1988.

First published in 2002
by Hodder Children's Books,
a division of Hodder Headline Limited,
338 Euston Road, London NW1 3BH

10 9 8 7 6 5 4 3 2 1

Printed in Hong Kong

All rights reserved

Bearum Scarum

written by
VIC PARKER

illustrated by
EMILY BOLAM

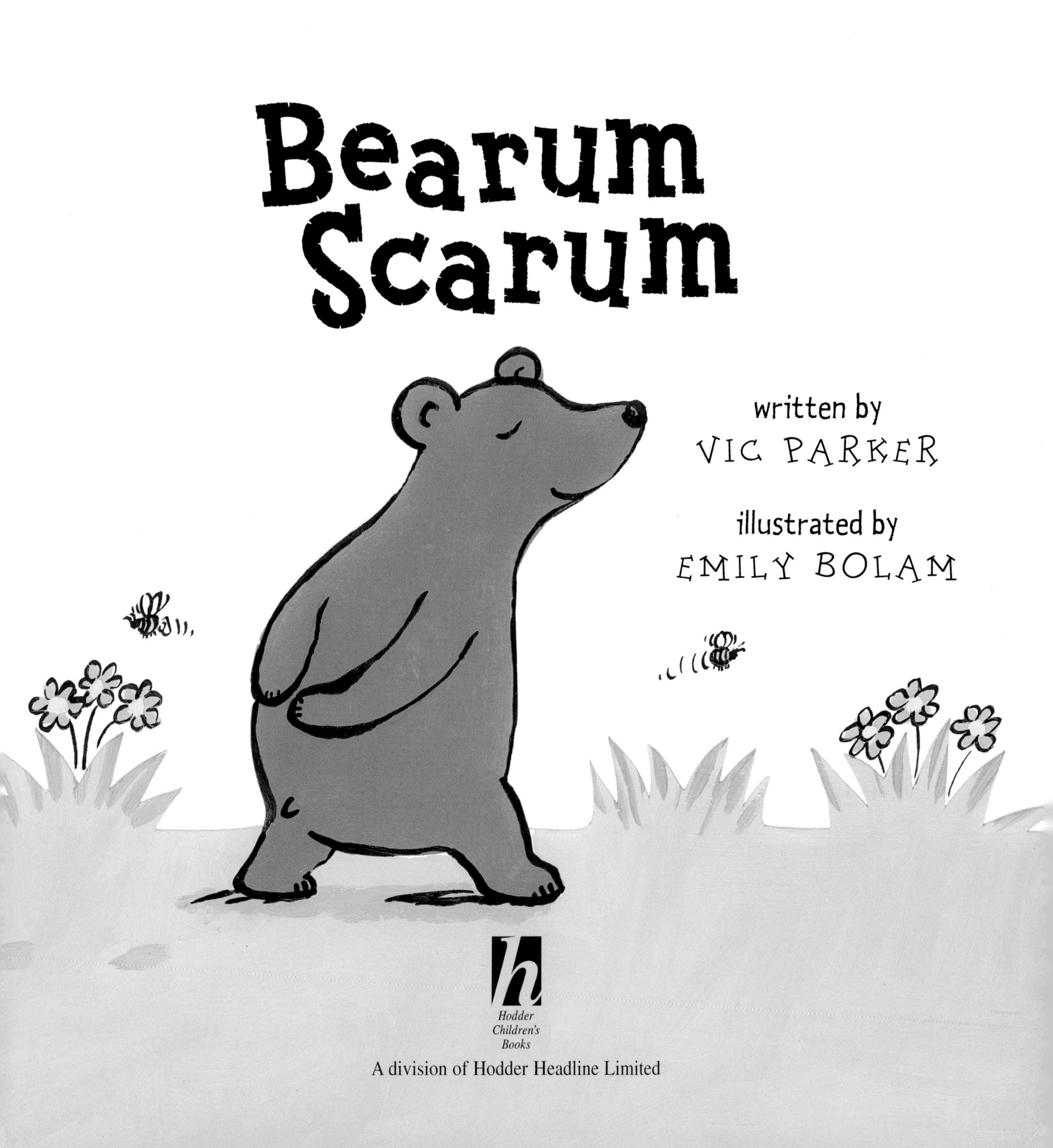

Hodder Children's Books
A division of Hodder Headline Limited

Ten hairy hunters are out to find a bear.
Ten hairy hunters are searching everywhere.
Ten hairy hunters discover Bear's tracks . . .

Shhh!

Bear's friends are right behind their backs.

Ten hairy hunters start following the trail.
Ten hairy hunters are hot on Bear's tail.
Ten hairy hunters head into the unknown.

Shhh! Bear's friends do some hunting of their own.

Nine hairy hunters at the edge of a ridge.
Nine hairy hunters see there isn't any bridge.
Nine hairy hunters swing across the gap.

Shhh! Bear's friends smuggle off another chap.

Eight hairy hunters reach a muddy bog.
Eight hairy hunters balance on a log.
Eight hairy hunters wobble on their way.

Shhh! Bear's friends steal another man today.

Seven hairy hunters come to a sudden stop.
Seven hairy hunters peer up at the top.
Seven hairy hunters climb towards the sun.

Shhh! Bear's friends carry off another one.

Six hairy hunters dig a deep, dark pit.
Six hairy hunters bring some leaves to cover it.
Six hairy hunters make a trap to catch Bear.

Shhh! Bear's friends have set their own snare . . .

Five hairy hunters have to take a little swim.
Five hairy hunters hold their breath and jump in.
Five hairy hunters splash towards the other side.

Shhh! Bear's friends float one off on the tide.

Four hairy hunters take a tunnel through the trees.
Four hairy hunters crawl low on hands and knees.
Four hairy hunters squeeze along to reach the light.

Shhh! Bear's friends snatch another out of sight.

Three hairy hunters set some bait.
Three hairy hunters lie in wait.
Three hairy hunters start to snore.

Shhh! Bear's friends get rid of one more.

ZZZZ
HONEY

Two hairy hunters go creeping up on Bear.
Two hairy hunters don't want Bear to know they're there.
Two hairy hunters are sneaking very near.

Shhh! Bear's friends make one hunter disappear.

One hairy hunter comes face to face with Bear.
One hairy hunter thinks he's got Bear fair and square.
One hairy hunter looks deep into Bear's eyes.

One hairy hunter gets a **big** surprise –

Arrgghhhh!

No hairy hunters left – they're all off on the run
No hairy hunters left – Bear and his friends have won.
No hairy hunters left – Bear puts a sign on view:

KEEP OUT
YOU HAIRY HUNTERS
OR WE'LL
BEARUM SCARUM YOU!